This book belongs to
my friend:
DESTYN

A NOTE TO PARENTS

Children of all ages love animals. From household pets and farm animals to the fascinating creatures of the wild, it is always exciting to learn what makes each type of animal unique. In *Blue's Safari Skidoo*, Blue and her friends go on a safari and gather interesting facts about many of the animals they meet.

As you read the story, spend some time on each page talking about the featured animal. What is its name? What makes it special? How do the animals differ from one another? Look for other animals in the backgrounds that are part of the African landscape. Make sure to point out that each animal has its own special place in the animal kingdom. Before Blue learns the answer to the book's overriding question, ask your child to guess what the biggest land animal is.

The next time you are planning an outing, consider exploring your local zoo or petting park. After your adventure, help your child make his own animal scrapbook, just like Blue! Use old magazines and newspapers plus colorful papers and crayons. Encourage your child to highlight his favorites. Include some informational tidbits about each animal. Your child's animal scrapbook will be a fun and informative memory-keeper to return to again and again.

Learning Fundamental: 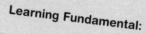 **science**

For more parent and kid-friendly activities, go to www.nickjr.com.

Blue's
Safari Skidoo

Published by Scholastic Inc., 90 Old Sherman Turnpike, Danbury, CT 06816

SCHOLASTIC and associated logos are trademarks and/or registered trademarks of Scholastic Inc.

ISBN 0-7172-6625-7

Printed in the U.S.A.

First Scholastic Printing, December 2002

Blue's Safari Skidoo

by
Kitty Fross

illustrated by
Victoria Miller

SCHOLASTIC INC.

New York Toronto London Auckland Sydney
Mexico City New Delhi Hong Kong Buenos Aires

"What are you doing, Blue?" Periwinkle asked, as he strolled into Blue's room.

"I'm making an animal scrapbook," Blue answered. "Look, here's a whale. It's the biggest animal in the sea!"

"Neat!" said Periwinkle. "What's the biggest
animal on land?"
Blue scratched her head. "I'm not sure."

"How can we find out?" asked Periwinkle.
"Let's talk to some animals," Blue said. "Follow me!"
Quick as a wink, Blue bounded into her scrapbook.

"Blue skidoo, you can, too!" she called.
Periwinkle took a deep breath and jumped in
after Blue. "Blue skidoo, I can, too!" he sang, as
he spun around and around.

Periwinkle and Blue landed on a soft grassy slope. A big gray animal was standing nearby. When he saw them, he ran over, his huge ears flapping with every step.

"Hi there," the animal called. "I'm Baby Elephant.
Are you here on a safari?"

"What's a safari?" asked Periwinkle.

"It's a trip to see animals," Baby Elephant explained.

"That's just what we want to do!" Blue said excitedly.

"Do you know who the biggest animal on land is?"

"Of course!" said Baby Elephant. "I can take you to meet him."

"Great!" said Blue. "Let's go!"

"Go, go, go! That's what I like to hear!" purred
a big cat as she stepped out of the grass.

"Who are you?" asked Periwinkle.

"I'm Cheetah," the cat replied. "I'm the fastest
animal on Earth!"

"Wow!" said Blue.

"I'd love to stay and chat," said Cheetah, "but I've got to run. Enjoy your safari."

"Bye!" they called. But Cheetah was already out of sight.

They followed Baby Elephant to a forest, where a brightly colored animal stood among the trees.

"Hi, Mandrill!" said Baby Elephant. "My friends are here to meet the biggest animal."

"Well, I'm not the biggest," Mandrill replied. "But I

do have a very big family. I have eight-hundred aunts, cousins, sisters, and brothers!"

"Wow! That is a big family," said Blue.

"Enjoy your visit with the biggest animal!" Mandrill said, winking at Baby Elephant.

Baby Elephant led them to the river. A large animal was rolling happily on the bank, singing to himself. "Hello!" he called out cheerfully. "It's hot out there. Come wallow in the mud to keep cool!"

"We'd love to, Warthog, but my friends
are searching for the biggest animal," Baby
Elephant explained.

"You sure have big teeth!" Blue said to Warthog.
Warthog laughed. "Those are tusks. I use them
for digging."

"And someday my tusks will be much bigger than
his!" Baby Elephant crowed.

"Yes, yes, Baby Elephant,"
Warthog said with a smile. "Someday."
   "Want to check out the lake?"
Baby Elephant asked.
   "Sure!" said Blue and Periwinkle.
"Nice to meet you, Warthog!"

On the lake's surface, a pair of huge eyes blinked.
Then a massive head rose from the water.

"There's Hippopotamus," whispered Baby Elephant.

Periwinkle cleared his throat. "Excuse me, are you
the biggest animal?"

"No," Hippopotamus grunted. Then with a giant
yawn, she sank back under the water.

"Well, that's the biggest *mouth* you'll see on your
safari," Baby Elephant giggled.

"Don't mind Hippo," twittered a bird standing nearby.

"Oh, hello," said Blue. "Hey, your beak is shaped like a spoon!"

"That's why they call me Spoonbill," the bird explained. "I use it for catching fish."

Spoonbill dipped his beak into the lake and came up holding a fish.

"Nice catch!" cheered Periwinkle.

"Let's head back to the grassland," Baby Elephant suggested. "See you, Spoonbill!"

When they arrived at the grassland, they saw a
very tall animal eating leaves off the top of a tree.

"You must be the biggest animal!" Blue shouted up
to her. "What's your name?"

"I'm Giraffe," the animal replied. "I'm not the biggest, but I am the tallest. And I have the longest neck!"

"Well, if you're not the biggest, who is?" asked Periwinkle.

Baby Elephant made a trumpeting sound with his trunk. "Surprise!" he said. "I'm the biggest animal!"

"How can you be the biggest?" asked Blue. "We met lots of animals bigger than you."

"Just wait a few years," said Baby Elephant.
"Then you'll see."
"That's right, son," said a voice behind them.

Blue and Periwinkle looked up. There stood the
biggest animal they had seen on their whole safari.
"So you're the biggest animal!" Blue exclaimed.
"I'm the biggest animal on land," Papa Elephant
said with a nod.

"And someday, Baby Elephant will be just as big as I am!" Papa Elephant said proudly.

"Or even bigger!" Baby Elephant crowed, tapping his father's trunk gently with his own.

"What a great safari!" said Blue.

"It was Peri-perfect!" Periwinkle agreed.

"Thanks for showing us around, Baby Elephant!"

Blue looked at Periwinkle. "I guess it's time to go home," she said.

"Blue skidoo, we can, too!" they sang as they whirled around and around.

Periwinkle and Blue landed back in Blue's bedroom. Blue picked up her scrapbook and carefully pasted in a new picture.

"Bye-bye," she whispered to the picture.

"See you around!" said Periwinkle.

And from the pages of Blue's scrapbook, the biggest animal on land winked back at them.